My SELF Bookshelf

Who's Coming Tonight?

By JeongIm Choi

Illustrated by MinJeong Gang

Language Arts Consultant: Joy Cowley

NORWOOD HOUSE PRESS

Chicago, Illinois

DEAR CAREGIVER MySELF Bookshelf is a series of books that support children's social emotional learning. SEL has been proven to promote not only the development of self-awareness, responsibility, and positive relationships, but also academic achievement.

Current research reveals that the part of the brain that manages emotion is directly connected to the part of the brain that is used in cognitive tasks, such as: problem solving, logic, reasoning, and critical thinking—all of which are at the heart of learning.

SEL is also directly linked to what are referred to as 21st Century Skills: collaboration, communication, creativity, and critical thinking. MySELF Bookshelf offers an early start that will help children build the competencies for success in school and life.

In these delightful books, young children practice early reading skills while learning how to manage their own feelings and how to be considerate of other perspectives. Each book focuses on aspects of SEL that help children develop social competence that will benefit them in their relationships with others as well as in their school success. The charming characters in the stories model positive traits such as: responsibility, goal setting, determination, patience, and celebrating differences. At the end of each story, you will find a letter that highlights the positive traits and an activity or discussion to help your child apply SEL to his or her own life.

Above all, the most important part of the reading experience is to have fun and enjoy it!

Sincerely,

Shannon Cannon

Shannon Cannon, Ph.D.
Literacy and SEL Consultant

Norwood House Press • P.O. Box 316598 • Chicago, Illinois 60631
For more information about Norwood House Press please visit our website at www.norwoodhousepress.com or call 866-565-2900.

Shannon Cannon—Literacy and SEL Consultant
Joy Cowley—English Language Arts Consultant
Mary Lindeen—Consulting Editor

Library of Congress Cataloging-in-Publication Data
    Choi, Jeongim.
    Who's coming tonight? / by JeongIm Choi ; illustrated by MinJeong Gang.
      pages cm. -- (Myself bookshelf)
    Summary: "When the mean Red Fox plans on stealing the ducks on the lake, three ducks work together to protect and keep their friends safe. Concepts include responsibility and bravery"-- Provided by publisher. ISBN 978-1-59953-653-8 (library edition : alk. paper) -- ISBN 978-1-60357-675-8 ebook) [1. Courage--Fiction. 2. Responsibility--Fiction. 3. Foxes--Fiction. 4. Ducks--Fiction.] I. Gang, MinJeong, illustrator. II. Title. III. Title: Who's coming tonight?
    PZ7.C446257Who 2014
    [E]--dc23
                      2014009403

Manufactured in the United States of America in Stevens Point, Wisconsin.
252N—072014

Who's Coming Tonight?

Autumn came to the little lake.
The ducks were swimming
and the leaves were falling.
All was peaceful and calm.

4

Then, one day, a wild goose flew in.
"Be careful!" the goose warned.
"An evil red fox is in the forest."

The ducks quacked with fear.
Would the evil red fox eat them?

They saw a letter on a leaf,
tacked to the bark of a tree.
That letter made their feathers
stand on end.

I'm coming
tonight!
Red Fox

The ducks had a meeting
and made a plan.
"We can't all stay awake.
We need three sentries
who will wake us up
when the fox appears."

So three young strong ducks
were chosen to stay awake
all night, on sentry duty.

9

Night fell and the lake was dark.
The three sentries said,
"We will guard the lake
without blinking our eyes,
without nodding off."

That's how they stood all night,
their eyes wide open.
But the evil red fox
did not come that night.

The next night,
the three ducks guarded the lake.
They blinked their eyes
and nodded off.
The fox did not come.

On the third night,
the ducks were so tired
they went to a swamp and slept.

13

When they woke up
and went back to the lake,
it was empty!
The fox had been there!

The ducks were upset. They quacked,
"This happened because we neglected
our sentry duty. We need a plan
to rescue all our friends
from the evil red fox."

They put their heads together.
Then they wrote on a leaf:
We're coming tonight!
Three Ducks

When the red fox saw the note,
he sneered. "Silly ducks!
They are copying my trick!
I'll catch them and eat them all!"

Night fell, and the red fox waited,
not moving an inch,
for the three ducks.

The next night, the red fox
did not blink his eyes
nor did he nod off.

20

On the third night,
he still kept his eyes wide open.

On the fourth morning,
his bloodshot eyes closed.
"I have to get some sleep
to get ready for tonight,"
he mumbled.

Snore, snore, snore.

While the fox's snores
echoed through the forest,
the three ducks rescued
all the ducks in the fox's net.

Then they cast the net
over the sleeping fox.

Some wild geese flying south
picked up the fox in the net.
They would take him far away
from the forest.

24

Thanks to the three ducks,
the evil red fox was gone.
The ducks swam on the lake.
The autumn leaves fell.
All was peaceful and calm again.

Dear Three Brave Ducks,

Thank you for saving us from the evil red fox.

You tried to guard us every night,

and we understand that you got tired when the red fox did not show up.

However, when the fox took us all, you came to save us.

Although there was great danger, you acted in a responsible way.

You are the brave peacekeepers of our beautiful lake.

From the grateful ducks

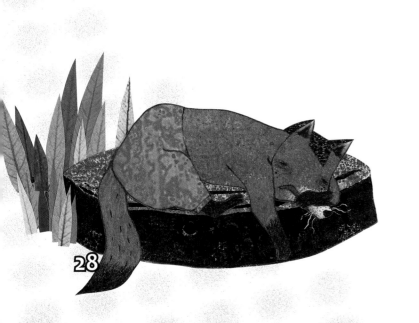

28

SOCIAL AND EMOTIONAL LEARNING FOCUS

Responsibility

The three brave ducks acted responsibly when the red fox tricked them. The rest of the ducks were grateful that they made a plan to rescue them. The three ducks took responsibility for falling asleep and neglecting their duty to keep watch over the lake.

On a sheet of paper, make a list of all of the things you are responsible for such as, cleaning your room, walking the dog, feeding the cat, doing your homework, or emptying the trash. You can make a "Responsibilitree" to remind you of your duties:

- Draw a picture of a bare tree.

- Cut out pieces of paper in the shapes of leaves.

- Write each responsibility on separate leaves.

- Color the tree and the leaves.

- Glue the leaves to the tree picture.

You can make a "Family Responsibilitree" by labeling the branches with each family member's name on a branch. Then, create the leaves and glue them to each person's branch to show how your family works together by taking responsibility.

Reader's Theater

Reader's Theater is an interactive approach to reading that allows students to understand each story through dramatic interpretation. By involving students in reading, listening, and speaking activities, they provide an integrated approach for students to develop fluency and comprehension. A Reader's Theater edition of this book is available online. You can access the script by scanning the QR code to the right or visit our website at: http://www.norwoodhousepress.com/whoscomingtonight.aspx